Thank you, Johanna Hurley

SIMON & SCHUSTER BOOKS FOR YOUNG READERS
An imprint of Simon & Schuster Children's Publishing Division
1230 Avenue of the Americas, New York, New York 10020
© 2022 by Rosemary Wells
Book design by Laurent Linn © 2022 by Simon & Schuster, Inc.
The author would like to add the following thank-you: Thank you to Daniela Nyberg (Bulgarian Cultural and Heritage Center of Seattle)
and Michele Anciaux Aoki at the University of Washington, Slavic Languages & Literature Department, for their help with the Bulgarian translations.
All rights reserved, including the right of reproduction in whole or in part in any form.
SIMON & SCHUSTER BOOKS FOR YOUNG READERS and related marks are trademarks of Simon & Schuster, Inc.
For information about special discounts for bulk purchases, please contact Simon & Schuster Special Sales
at 1-866-506-1949 or business@simonandschuster.com.
The Simon & Schuster Speakers Bureau can bring authors to your live event. For more information or to book an event,
contact the Simon & Schuster Speakers Bureau at 1-866-248-3049 or visit our website at www.simonspeakers.com.
The text for this book was set in Family Dog.
The illustrations for this book were rendered in watercolor and ink.
Manufactured in China
0522 SCP
First Edition
2 4 6 8 10 9 7 5 3 1
Library of Congress Cataloging-in-Publication Data
Names: Wells, Rosemary, author, illustrator.
Title: Max can read! / Rosemary Wells.
Description: First edition. | New York : Simon & Schuster Books for Young Readers, [2022] | Series: A Max and Ruby adventure | "A Paula Wiseman Book." | Audience: Ages 4–8. |
Audience: Grades K–1. | Summary: Max figures out how to assemble his new gift even though the instructions for putting it together are written in Bulgarian.
Identifiers: LCCN 2021047429 (print) | LCCN 2021047430 (ebook) | ISBN 9781534493964 (hardcover) | ISBN 9781534493971 (ebook)
Subjects: LCSH: Reading—Juvenile fiction. | Rabbits—Juvenile fiction. | CYAC: Reading—Fiction. | Rabbits—Fiction. | LCGFT: Picture books.
Classification: LCC PZ7.W46843 Marsw 2022 (print) | LCC PZ7.W46843 (ebook) | DDC [E]—dc23
LC record available at https://lccn.loc.gov/2021047429
LC ebook record available at https://lccn.loc.gov/2021047430

Max & Ruby

MAX CAN READ!

ROSEMARY WELLS

A Paula Wiseman Book

SIMON & SCHUSTER BOOKS FOR YOUNG READERS

New York   London   Toronto   Sydney   New Delhi

One day the mail carrier brought a **big** package
to Max and Ruby's house.
It came all the way from Uncle Gyorgy in Bulgaria.

Inside were two boxes.
"Happy Valentine!" said Max.

"No, Max," said Max's sister, Ruby.
"The picture on the card says
'Happy Double Birthday, Macks and Rubi!'"

Ruby's present was a **crystal growing kit**.
Ruby set up her laboratory in the kitchen.
"Crystals are easy," said Ruby. "We had them in science."

Max opened his present.
Inside was an **air-powered jet-pack space suit**
in a hundred pieces.
But Max could not read the instruction book.
How was Max to put the space suit together?

Max wanted help with his space suit.
"Find the words in your *Reading Is Fun* book,
Max," said Ruby. "Right now I'm going to activate
the Mr. Bunsen Safety Warmer. Then I'm going to
drip ten drops of red fluid into this beaker."

Max looked for space suit words in his *Reading Is Fun* book, but he could not find them. Max still wanted help.
"In a minute," said Ruby.

"Look, Max," said Ruby. "My red cobra crystal
is going to take over the kitchen!"
Max went back to *Reading Is Fun*.

But there were **no** space suit words **anywhere** in
Reading Is Fun. Max wanted help again.
"I'm switching over to a yellow cyclops crystal, Max," said Ruby.
"You'll have to wait. It's a delicate moment."

Max waited until the yellow crystal crystalized.
Just then Ruby began preparing for a blue dragon crystal.
"I've got three crystals going at once, Max," said Ruby.
"You're on your own!"

Max placed the hundred-piece space suit back into its box.
He took it over to Grandma's house.

Grandma loved Uncle Gyorgy.
She was thrilled to work on his present.

"**Oh, dear,**" said Grandma.
"These instructions are written in **Bulgarian**.
I can't read Bulgarian. We will have to go to the library
and send for a Bulgarian dictionary on interlibrary loan."
Max knew that would take all summer to happen.

Max folded up the instruction book. Suddenly, he noticed something he had missed before. In the back of the book were how-to put-together pictures of the space suit. There were **loads of pictures**.

Max could read those pictures.

Max had no trouble inserting the
eyelets for the space boot laces.

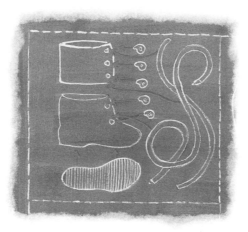

Then he attached the soles and
began working on the gravity gloves.

Every tiny detail was
in the pictures.

Grandma got the front zipper going, and Max Velcroed
the dehydrated-food pockets to the legs of the suit.

Last came the helmet. Attaching the voice-to-base earphones was a no-brainer.

The visor clamped on with a solid click.
Max got in and zipped up the front.

Once assembled, the jet-pack air pump worked perfectly.

Max bounced home.

Ruby had just finished a lunch-box-size purple crystal.
"**Max!**" said Ruby. "**You did it!**
You learned to read the instructions!"

"I can read!" said Max.
"It's easy! Even in Bulgarian!"

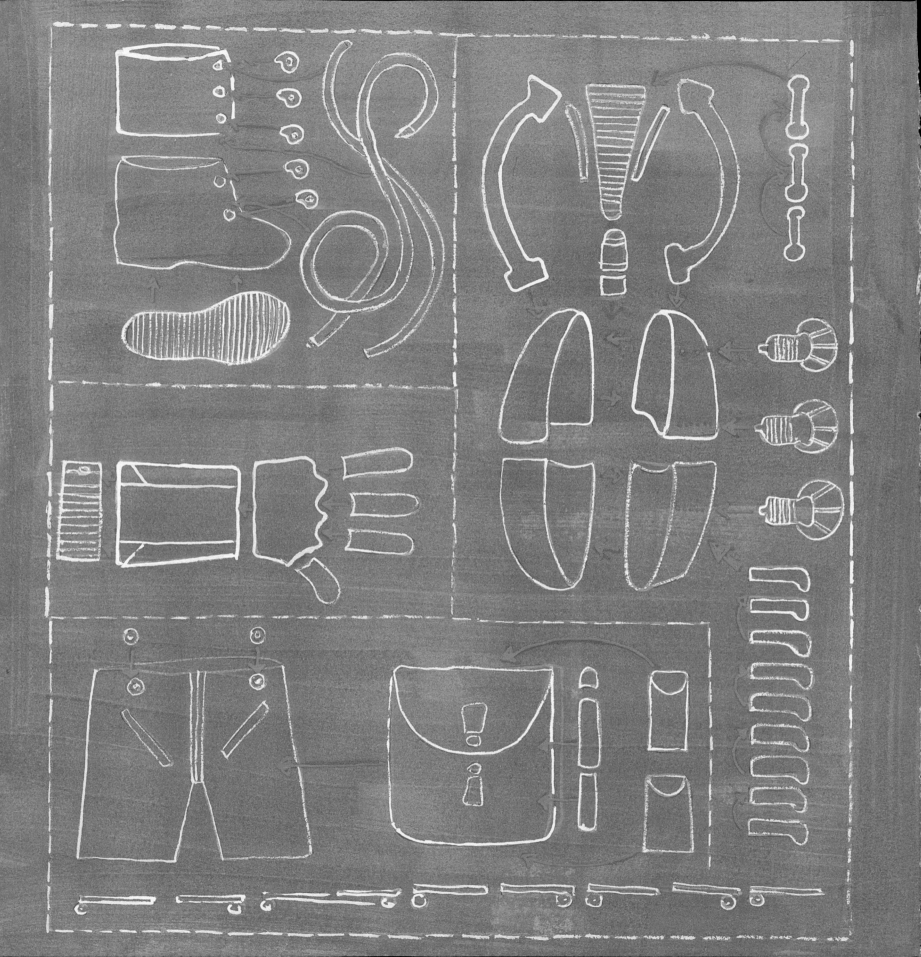